AF488107

Paul Riley Hot Wives 1
Copyright (C) 2022
By Paul Riley

First printing, 2022.

ISBN: 9798446506712
Imprint: Independently published

Author Notes and Warnings: All characters in this story are 18 years and older, this is a work of fiction and as such do not try this on your own.

Paul Riley Hot Wives 1

Aasta Becomes a Hotwife

My name is Aasta, and I am heading over to an adult bookstore, to become a sexy little slut like my husband wishes for me to become, as this will be my first time going to an adult bookstore and using their gloryhole for my own entertainment as I will be the main course.

My husband told me which adult video store to go too, and a stall is already for me to use once I am there. All I need to do is, tell the clerk who I am and that things have been setup for me, and I will be setup with the room that is ready for me.

So right now, I am on my way there now, as I have everything I will need, as I am wearing a slut outfit, as I make my way to the location where I need to head too, as I drive, I look around. I do this as I wanted to look for spots to maybe have sex outside with random dudes who need to bust a nut into someone. However, this is for another time, and as for now I need to learn to become a good hotwife not only for my husband but for other men as well, as I will allow them to even impregnate me, I want them to know that my holes are theirs to use as they please and I am their little slut and as such they can fuck me how they see fit.

While I was looking around, I came to a bridge that I have to go under anyways to reach my location, I saw a couple of homeless men, that looked like they needed someone to have some good times with, I sighed as I have a choice should I go to the bookstore or have random sex, which is a fantasy of mine.

The truth yes, I will have random sex so to speak however these men are men that my husband has chosen for me, ahead of time, and the truth is the store is open 24 hours, and the night is still young, also my husband gave me no clear time to go there as he said I can take my time, but it has to happen tonight.

I need to make up my mind fast as I am coming up to the point, I need to either head to the adult bookstore or have some fun beforehand. I decided to go ahead and have sex, as these men will be my first practice and as such the feeling of cum inside of me, as I am at the bookstore started to turn me on a bit more.

Finding a spot that I could safety park and then head back to was not that hard as I decided to park near to them, and as I pulled up to them, they looked at me, I then have a choice now, I can at any moment decided to not go with this, or I can go with this.

I have decided to go ahead and do what I wanted to do, as I pulled up and stopped the car, the men than started to approach me, they came over to me and I rolled down the window and I asked, "Do you guys want to have a good time for a while?"

"We are broke, but yes we would love to fuck you miss!" One of them answered me, as I could see that they were not the cleanest of men, but I don't care right now, I want to work on my sexual side of myself.

I than said to them with a smile, "I am not some whore, or hooker, in fact I will ask of you a favor, if you all want to help me out and I will help you all out."

I got their attention as the one that I would say is the leader then asked me, "Ok you got our attention so what is it that you wish for us to do?"

"I want the four of you to be willing to fuck me, whenever and I will provide you your own place and food and a better place then this bridge unless you like it here." I said to them,

They looked at each other and then smiled and asked me, "You have to have money miss or some sex craze bitch."

I sighed as I than pulled out my purse and I got out two thousand dollars' worth of bills and handed it to them. They took it as they knew that I am now for real as he than said to me, "Fine we believe you this is more than what we got in a couple of months."

I completely stop the car, as I then took the keys out and I put the keys around my neck as I had a necklace for my keys, and I got out of the car, I then took off my clothes and throw them into the car, now naked I closed the door.

Both surprise and turned on at what I did they looked at me and the leader asked, "Shouldn't we do this somewhere else?"

"Is this where you sleep?" I asked.

He then answered me and said, "Yes."
I smiled as I than asked, "Well show me where the four of you sleep here and you four can gangbang me."

They smiled as they lead me over to where they sleep, as they all started to get naked themselves. I was standing as they got themselves hard as one of them laid down on the bed, I went over him as I slowly went down on top him as he keeps his cock hard as it slowly entered my pussy.

Panting with both excitement and lust as his cock entered me, as it slowly went deeper into me, as I took a cock who may have fucked whatever and I could get something which excited me even more.

As I lowered myself even more, as my hungry pussy took more and more of the man's cock, he than said, "Damn woman your pussy is so tight, and I am loving this!"

"Let me take all of you inside and that goes with all of you fuck me tonight we have enough time, for this, but you do not have me the whole night though." I said, as I started to moan with every bit more, he worked himself into my pussy.

After a bit more, I was completely on top of him and his cock is completely inside of me, which even more excited me, as I have my first man inside of me that is not my husband, as I bounce on his cock slowly to get use to him as I put my hands onto my breast as I squeeze on them as I bounce on him.

He soon took my hands as he started to squeeze them as I went down on him as we started to kiss as he took me, pounding my pussy as deep as he could as I could taste his breathe which for some reason is making me even more turned on even though he smelled of alcohol which would have turned my stomach a while ago but now I feel even more of a slut as I am having a drunk fuck me.

At that moment as the two of us were fucking as two firm hands took hold of my butt, on both sides as they were spread apart, I thought to myself, "OH God he is going to fuck my ass!"

After I realizes that, I started to even get more excited as a orgasm is coming for me soon, and it did once his cock's head is now at the opening of my ass, as he slowly slides himself into me, at that moment he went deep into me, and started to pound my pussy without lube or without care as he did so, I didn't even notice the pain at the moment only the lust as I have two men fucking me.

Soon, another man, took my head off of the man below me as he slammed his cock deep down my throat, this excited me too much as I orgasm as he throats fuck me as I am now being made into the slut and whore which my husband wished me to become.

I couldn't moan or scream load, but I was moaning as well as I could as I had all three holes being fucked, soon I started to feel as the three men started to empty themselves into my holes, and soon the taste of cum was in my mouth.

After a bit the two men that were in my ass and mouth went back to their makeshift beds, as I got up from the man that I was on top of, as I have one more man to please. As I got up, I saw he was ready and waiting for me to get done, so I went on all fours, and wiggled my ass and pussy at him which is still very much dripping cum from the two other men.

I looked back and I asked, "Want to fuck me like a bitch in heat, I am your bitch fuck me!"

So, he came over to me, as I looked in front of me, as I felt the head of his cock enter my pussy, soon he started to pound my pussy hard and deep as I moaned and panted. Soon he started to come into me, unable to hold onto his cum like the others as he was, I am sure building up loads to empty into a woman.

After he came into my pussy, he stayed in me for a bit as he enjoyed my cunt, afterwards once he knew he fully came inside of me, he pulled out slowly and then he got up. Panting from my first gangbang I have ever had, as I than slowly got up.

The four homeless men were looking at me with a grin as they have all been relieve of a burden and is grateful of what I did. I than made sure I had my keys on my necklace, and they are still there, as I than went over to them.

"I will be back, I will pay you, however, please stay here I may come for another session of that." I said to them as I headed to the car.

They then smiled as I head to my car, and I unlocked it, once I was in the car, I then got out some more cash, which I then locked the door and headed back to them, I gave each one of them 2k each and they thank me for the money.

I then headed back to the car, I am not filled yet as I am craving more sex, I would have these men fuck me, again but I can tell that they are beat from my first gangbang, however I am not beat, and I want more.

Once I got to the car, I got dress and I then started the car again as I locked the door as I than started to go on my way, that is when my phone rang, I reach to see who is calling and it's my husband.

I answered and he asked, "Hi Aasta have you went to the bookstore yet?"

"Not yet, I had a detour." I answered him.

He then seemed a bit happy and said to me, "Well I wanted to let you know that it has to be postpone for now, as somethings have happened with some of the men that I have picked for you."

"Ah ok, well are you ok if I just have some my time, and explore a bit?" I asked, as if he would not mind, I know he would be fine with it.

He then said, "Do whatever you want to do, be my guest and have fun."

"Sounds good with me, I will of course be safe as always." I said, as the two of us then hanged up, after that I smiled as this gives me a much better chance of exploring things on my own, instead of having my husband setup things.

Smiling I saw a perfect spot to try out things as a local park comes up, one which is far from where I live and as such one that would be perfect to find someone or men to fuck me. So, I then looked for a parking lot to park in so I can explore the park.

Once I did, I then parked my car, and locked up everything but I also keep my keys on my necklace. My goal is to at least find maybe one or two men not at the same time, but one after the other. If it happens at the same time than more power for me.

Getting out of my car, as I have everything I need as I shut the door as I made sure I locked the car up, and before that made sure I have my keys. Which I did, which is a good thing, as I have nothing else with me.

As I started to walk around the park, I came across a man that is smoking at a bench, he has not notice me yet as I came up to him. Once I did, I asked him, "Mind if I sit down next to you?"

Surprise to hear another human's voice he turned around and saw it was me a woman, and he smiled as he said, "Sure you can sit next to me if you like."

"Thank you." I said, as I sat next to him.

He than asked me, "So what brings you out here, alone at night?"

"Well just getting some air and figured why not." I answered him with a seductive tone.

He then looked at me closer seeing that I am not wearing much, and his smile turned into a grin as he asked, "Are you looking for someone to meet you here, or just waiting for whatever?"

"Not looking for anyone, I just wanted to get some fresh air, and see what goes from there." I answered him.

He then asked me, "So you are into dogging aren't you, I can tell."

I smiled and asked, "Do you want to fuck me than?"

"Ah just the way I like them to the point and direct." He said, as he smiled more at me, as he asked, "If you are for real strip here."

So, I did just that, and he then said, "Kneel."

So, I did, as he stood him as I went over to his pants as he pulled his pants down and I took his cock as I started to suck on him till, he grows larger, then he said, "Ok now lean on the bench."

I got up and did so, as I felt his cock enter my pussy as he started to pound me, as he did so I moaned and panted as he fucked me, happy and excited as I am being fucked here in a strange park, by a stranger that I do not know.

"Like this don't you bitch?" He asked, as he reach around and played with my breast as he went over my naked back.

I said, with pants as he pounded my pussy, "Oh yes, yes, you fucking feel good, I want to be your bitch breed me, please!"

"You want my cum, Slut?" he asked,

Moaning more as I said, "Yes come inside of me, make me your bitch!"

He than started to pound me harder than he releases deep inside of me as he grunted as he came inside of me. He stayed on me for a bit as he regains his strength, as he is still inside me. Once his cock completely was drained inside of me, he than slowly got off of me as he did, he went pulled his pants up.

"That was a good fuck, man you are tight, but I can tell you had some action already, didn't you?" He asked me.

I smiled as I got up and I said, as I answered him, "Yes how did you tell, am I still wet and all?"

"Well yes, I can tell when someone had sex before it's called a sloppy second my dear." He said, as he spanked my ass as I turned around to gather my clothes up.

I smiled as he did so I asked, "Do want to fuck me again?"

"Um once for a night I am good, at least for now anyways." He answered me, then he said, "Well if you're looking for more, I am sure you will find one or two more but that will be it, at least for tonight anyways."

I smiled as I than said, "Thank you for the advice, I guess I will just carry my things than."

"That will be a good way to get more fucks depending on how you feel about certain things." He said, as I started to leave him as I travel on the path, naked as I carried my clothes with me.

I soon met two men, both drinking by a wooded area picnic area, which is both has light and also has a roof, for the rain etc. As I came near to them, one of them spots me and soon the two of them see me, come towards them.

Both of them raise to their feet and come over to me, I stop as I placed my clothes onto the ground as they started to touch and feel my naked body, as they did so I moaned and panted as they gently touch me.

Soon my pussy and ass are being probed by their fingers as they finger fuck me. After a bit they pulled their pants down as they then bend me over as I felt the head of one of their cocks enter my pussy as it did I open my mouth wide as I moaned and panted as he pounded my pussy, as this happened the other man, wanting my pussy also and not wanting to fuck my mouth waited as he jerked off, to make sure he is large enough to fuck me.

After a bit, I had to move against one of the support beams so that I could position myself without the fear of falling onto the concert below me. As he pounded my pussy, I than said, "Yes oh yes fuck me harder baby fuck me make me your slut! Come inside of me, the both of you!"

After I said that, he than keep fucking me, as he wanted to make me wet, as I neared another orgasm, as it started, I tighten up once more as he sprayed his seed into my insides. After he unloaded his load into me, he stayed inside of me loving the feeling that my pussy gives to him, then he came out of me with a slurping sound.

I then stayed like I was as the next man, then took the other's position as he wanted to really fuck me and nut inside of me. As he pounded my pussy I moan even louder as I did so, he fuck me harder and deeper as he wanted to make me sing to him as he fucked me.

Soon, like the first man he came deep inside of me, then he keeps fucking me as he loved me singing a tone of orgasms that he enjoyed. After a bit he stopped and the two of them got dress, as I then decided to go ahead and leave the park, and more likely head home.

After I was fully dress, I made it out of the park as I made my way back to my car. Once I got to my car, I than took off and headed back home, I am starting to get tired and I felt it was best to get some rest as I do need some sleep, as I can sense I will need it.

I felt for some reason to head back home, for some reason I felt that a wonderful sexual surprise awaits me, I also am getting a bit tired as well, so I am on my way back home. So, once I got home, I exited my car and I took with me everything I needed as I locked up, I then walked inside the home, and I was greeted by my husband, who seemed to be some what surprise to see me back at this time.

I smiled as I asked, "Is everything ok my dear?"

"Yes, it is, I just thought you won't be back this soon, I thought I would have some time to get things done before you came back home." He said with a grin.

I then grin in a playful way as I asked, "Were you planning something for me, as in a sexual surprise?"

"Well yes I was, however, you seemed to be well still wanting sex so well if you wait a bit, I will have everything setup for you." He said, as he added, "However if you would like to wait in the other room, while you wait for me to prepare for things for you."

I then smirk as I asked, "So how did you know that I had sex already with other men?"

"Easy I can smell the musk from the men that more likely flooded your womb with their seed, am I correct?" He answered me as he asked me.

I sigh with a smile as I answered him, "Yes I have had sex with seven men, and out of those I had my first threesome, and gangbang."

Smiling with favor for me, and realizing that I did well, he said, "I am proud of you than, you did well, and better than the adult store would have turned out, however I still wish for you to try out a glory hole, but that can be some other time."

"For now, I want you to relax as I do have something planned for you, something special that will help you have a time of your life." He said to me, as he put his arm around my waist as he led me to another room.

He then stopped for a moment seeing I still have my purse with me, and he said, "Here let me take your things with me and I will bring them to our bedroom, also if you wish you can strip here or wait."

I then gave him my purse which has my keys and I than also gave to him my necklace as I placed it in my purse, I then took off my clothes, now completely naked once more, as I handed him my clothes. He grins at me as he led me to the room that he has prepared for me a special sexual treat that I can sense that I will more than likely not only enjoy but love.

Once we got to the room, I saw that it was another large room that we used for special events as it is large enough to host a massive gangbang or massive orgy. There hanging from the ceiling is a sling ready for me, to use. Also, and most importantly are three well hung and muscle-bound men, all handsome and well-endowed for me.

My husband paid no care to the expense that he did to find men for me, as their cocks were more than choice cocks for me, as the three men came over to me, gently touching me, as my sexual excitement as well as theirs filled the room, as one of them went behind me as I felt his large cock rub against my naked skin and inches away from my ass or pussy.

He started to neck me as he tasted my skin as I slowly moved towards him as the two of us started to kiss. Soon the two other men, lifted me up from the ground and moved me over to the sling, as they did so the man behind me followed me till they placed me onto the sling.

Once there, they raise my arms as they bound my arms to the chains holding the sling up, as they did so, they prepared lifted my legs onto straps as they held my feet in place. My pussy and ass are wide open as my legs were spread apart well enough for one of them to use either hole.

"They will clean your pussy up with their mouths, and then they will fuck you, till they come, but I want to hear the sweet music of you being used so your mouth will be unused for now." He said, as he added, "So enjoy my prelude to things to come, my love."

He then left the room, as he shut the door behind me leaving me at the mercy of the three men that he chooses for me. Once he was gone, as I could see a clear view of where my pussy and ass are at, I can know when someone is there before I felt their cock or tongue inside of me. As one of them came in front of me and lower himself so that he was at the perfect height to start to eat my pussy or ass out.

He took his hands and place them firmly onto my legs as he pulled me into him, as I rolled my eyes as he went deep into me with his tongue as he tasted my sex as well as the seven men who came inside of me.

As he used his tongue to probe my pussy, he took one of his fingers to probe my ass, as he started to pound my ass with his large and thick finger as he licked and tasted my pussy. While he was licking me, he made sure to clean out my pussy, as he licked away the cum that is up and front.

Moaning as this is happening, I gasp hard onto the chains as he started to pound my ass as he ate me out, as with each thrust into my ass I would rock violently back and forth, moaning with each thrust and with each touch from his tongue, while he gave my insides of my vagina a bath, preparing me for them to have their turn to fuck me as well.

After a while as he made my moans, and pants into a song which all could hear well within our house, he soon stopped, as he raised up as his large cock is now able to be seen as he gently slapped it onto my stomach, I looked at him with a seductive grin, as he has a large grin on his face, showing his desire to pound my willing hole.

"Want to get breed slut?" he asked, as he slapped his cock gently onto my skin as he was before.

I smiled and said, "Oh yes fuck me, and impregnate me please oh God I love the way you three look, I want to have your babies!"

He smiled as he slides his whole cock into me, as he than started to pound me without mercy or regret as I started to pant and moan wildly, as he fine tunes me to start to sing him a song with my moans.

My cries and moans of pleasure was heard though out the house, as the room started to have the musk of sex, as the two other men, prepared themselves to also pound my pussy, and give me what I want more so.

While the first of the three men pound my pussy, as in he fucked me slowly and hard with each thrust into me, as he did, he rocked me back and forth but keep himself inside of me deeply as he held onto me as his member was deep inside of me.

Soon he started to quickly fuck me but still hard and deep, as he started to grunt and moan himself, while I am moaning making music for him and to the other two men in the room. I than felt as he started to spray his load inside of me, as he pulled me even more into him making sure that all of his seed is inside of my womb.

He stayed in me, for a bit as he finished up, and then he sighs as he went out of me and left me as he went to a bench that they were sitting before, I think. It did not take long for the next man to take his places, as it excited him to feel that my pussy is well used but still tight like that of a virgin on her first night of sex.

Doing the same thing that the first man did, he pounded me, as the slut that I am, as he does so, he listens to me sing to him, with my voice, as he pounds me, I soon orgasm making new music for him and the others to listen to as he fucks me.

After a bit he started to pound me faster but not harder, but still deeply inside of me, soon he started to grunt and moan, as he neared the moment of also coming deeply inside of me. Which came as I felt as he made sure he is deeply in me, as I felt him pumping his seed into me.

Sighing with that of pleasure and lust, as well as panting, I am having a blast as these three men fucked me, while my husband prepares something more for me to do. Thinking of this, as the next and last man entered me, sent me into another orgasm, as I once more sung the music of sex, as I rolled my eyes back, while I grasp hard to the chains as he pounded me.

While I have an orgasm, the last man is pounding me slowly as he is enjoying the tightness and feelings that my pussy is giving his cock, as it squeezes onto his cock, making it feel to him as a glove for his cock.

Moaning and panting as I return from my orgasm, I still am singing to them but with the tone I was before my orgasms, even if not as beautiful is something good to listen too, as he pounds my pussy.

However, he is nearing the point of coming inside of me, and that moment has come as he started to pull me into him as I started to feel as he started to pump his sperm inside of me. Moaning loudly, as he comes inside of me, he then went on and started to fuck me once more this time, harder and faster even as he is still coming into me.

"I want to fuck you and make you pregnant, I want to see your pregnant belly slut!" he said, as he once more started to fuck me.

As he fucked me for a while, the other two men, looked at what is happened as I turned towards them as they jerk off to what is happening, enjoying the show, knowing full well what my pussy feels like as they too have also added to the sperm inside of me.

Rolling my eyes once more as I started to have another orgasm once more, I have now last count as I have not experienced this level of pleasure like this before, and I have to feeling this will become the new normal for myself.

Singing even louder as he pounded me for what seemed like forever however, I cared not. As he is making me feel like the slut and hotwife that I wanted to become, however like all things he is nearing the point of coming deep inside of me.

Which came of course, as he pulled me into him as he pushed with all of his might into me, as he unloaded into me, while he did so he grunted as I moaned with another orgasm, yet again. While he filled my pussy with another load of his warm hot sperm, I felt well used now, given everything that has happened so far.

He finished inside of me, as he came out of me, with a slurping sound, as he did the extra sperm that was not in my uterus started to pour onto the floor below me, while I panted from all of the excitement that has just happened to me. Feeling well used and happy with this surprise it only makes me wonder what other surprises my husband has for me?

After a bit as they recover from fucking me, they got dress as they did so they saw me in the afterglow of sex, smiling at me, as I smiled at them, as I loved this every moment of it, my pussy is well feed, however it is still hungry for more.

Once they were done, they than came over to me, and untied me as they help me on my feet as they helped me sit down as I am panting from the afterglow of the sex, I just had with them.

Once I am sitting down, they waited for me to regain my strength as they motion me for my hand as they helped me to my feet as they started to walk me out of the room, even while naked still.

I could tell that they are now taking me to the next room, which is our bedroom. There I could hear the voices of many men, waiting to have a turn with me. I grinned and smiled as my body started to grow even more excited once again as I know what may befall me, as I believe I will have another gangbang, but in our bedroom.

Once we got to the bedroom door, one of them opened it for me, as I walked inside as I did, I saw about six other men, all about the same as in cock size, which is average. Now given the fact that I just had sex with three well-endowed men, and they fucked me good, this is a bit of a relief in some ways, as if I had six men like that, I will be too sore afterwards to do anything for maybe at most a week or longer.

I then saw what my husband is planning for me to do, as there are leg restraints to hold my legs up as my arms and hands will be free, as my husband then comes over to us as he is excited to see that I had my fair share of the fun and understand somewhat what is going on and what I will be doing soon.

My husband then helped me onto the bed as he got me comfortable as he then tied my ankles into place, as both of my legs are spread out given easy access to my pussy and ass, as the rest of my body is resting comfortably onto the bed, as the three men that did me before left the room, as my husband went out with them to talk with them.

He then came back as he then said as he shut the door, as he reentered the room, he then said as he shut the door behind him, "Her only hole that you can fuck with your cocks is her cunt, her mouth and ass are off limits for now, next time her whole body will be yours to use as you please."

They smiled and nodded as they moved into a line, as my husband also got naked and then got onto the bed first as he moved next to me, as he said, "Now listen to me, Aasta what we are going to do is we hug and kiss as they fuck you ok?"

Smiling and excited as this will be sexy and exciting as my husband and I kiss as my pussy is being fucked right in front of him. Growing more turned on and excited for what is about to happen, as the two of us started to kiss has I used my arms to raise up as my husband moves over my body as the two of us locked our eyes and then we started to kiss as our mouths touch as his tongue and my joined up.

Once this happened our eyes closed as I await the feelings to come, as we kissed and my husband played with my breast, I felt my pussy once more being tasted and licked as the man cleaned my pussy up, as he did, I moaned lightly as I couldn't make too much noise or sing like I did before, with my mouth and my husbands joined together as the two of us kiss, as we explored each other in our mouths while my pussy is being prepared to have yet another man fuck me.

After a bit as my body is being pleasured the man then stopped licking me as I felt as I could feel as his head of his cock is now at the opening of my pussy, as he slowly slides his cock deeply inside of me, as he does I moaned as loudly as I could, as now I had to stop kissing as I started to move my head and body back as I begun to once again, make music for all to hear me sing.

Once the man was completely inside of me, he then started to pound me pussy, knowing I can take it and knowing that I love it when a man fucks me hard and pounds me. While he fucks me, my husband then licks my upper body and makes me orgasm as my body is receive so much pleasure that it sent me over the edge.

After a bit of time, as my pussy tightens up as it does so it makes the man inside me love the feeling that this orgasm is giving to him, soon he starts to come deep inside of me, as I moan and cry out loud with lust as he pounds me, while he comes inside of me.

Didn't take that long till he finished up inside of me, as he then went out of me, as the next man, then didn't wait long as he started to fuck me once the first guy was out of me. While he fucked me, he went deep into me, well as deep as he could as he made sure his whole member went into me, as he did so, he fucked me.

"Oh, I am going o cum my little slut, I love your tight little pussy of yours, oh yes I am coming now!" He said to me, as he sprayed his warm, and wonderful cum deep inside my womb, as it is added to the others who have already came deep inside of me.

Staying inside of me, as he finishes up he then grinned at me, as he pulled out, once he has fully came inside of me, than the next man came forth as he went down on me as he started to lick and kiss my pussy, as he did so he started to lick and probe me with his tongue, as he started to greedily started to eat me out, which caused me a lot of pleasure as I moaned.

Loving the sound of my moans he made me sing to him with moans and cries till he stopped as his lips were dripping of salvia and my own juices. As he got up, he then slowly entered my pussy with his cock, and slowly entered me, as he presses forth into me.

Once he started to fuck me, he made me moan and as such sing to him once more, as I did so the other men that are left as I rolled my eyes as my mouth is wide open as I moaned as I give to them music from my moans. I saw as their cocks are preparing to fuck me as I smiled and got even more excited as I looked at my husband and smiled at him as I moved my hands to him as I touch his face as my body tumbled and rocked back and forth as I am being fucked.

I said, "Thank you so much for this, oh God I love this, I love being made to feel like a slut for you, I want so badly to have all of these men's babies if that is what you will for me, I love being fucked for you."

He smiled as he said, "Your welcome Aasta and I knew you would love this."

The two of us smiled as I touched his face, as I moaned as I am being fucked in front of him. Soon I orgasm once more as he shoots his load inside of me, making the number of men to come inside more then it was before. Now I have loss count of how many men have fucked me, as they have all came inside of me.

At this point I really do not care or I care less about how many people have fucked me, as it doesn't matter now at this point of time. After a bit, as the last of the men do me, its pretty much the same, as each of them could only fuck my pussy or lick it, as my pussy has had so many tongues and fingers inserted into it, let alone all the cocks that have fucked me, I should be sore, but I am not.

With each and every cock that fucks me it should by default help with my hungry for sex, yet for some reason it has not. In fact, with each cock that fucks me and comes inside of me, the hornier I become, which tells me yes, I have indeed become a slut for myself and my husband.

Too be honest this doesn't bother me, as I am enjoying myself, and the excitement this brings to me, as with the sex and attention that I get with each and every man that fucks me, even if they call me a bitch, a whore, or a slut, in many ways I am all of those, maybe not a whore but anyways the truth is I am loving being called these names.

Well, it didn't take long and the last of the men, have now fucked me and came deep inside of me. After he came inside of me, and left me there, my husband then got up and went and tied my arms up as my hands held tightly to the ropes that now bind my arms, as he had them out stretch as he rose up and then comes on top of me as his cock enters my very wet and moist cunt as he kisses me as he hold my hands as he fucks me.

Pounding my pussy, as he kisses, licks and sucks on my neck and mouth. As he sucks on my neck, making me have hickeys as he has his way with me, as now it is just him and me, as he keeps me. I love every moment of this, as he fucks me, as it excites me even more with each thrust into me, soon he comes deep inside of me.

Now panting and out of breath the two of us are tired as the two of us sleep together as is. Happy that my husband has made me into his little slut, and one that loves sex, and one that craves it with no end to how much I can have or need.

In the morning, we both woke up as he started to once more fuck me, and after he dealt with his morning wood, as in fucking me, and after he came inside of me. He then smiled as he untied me, and the two of us got up.

The two of us then headed over to the bathroom and went to take a shower as the men who had fucked me last night were brought outside and lead to their vehicles or given rides back to their homes.

Once the two of us were in the shower, which is one of those large ones, as the water starts, the two of us started to kiss as, we hold each other's hands as we were both next to each other as my pussy and his cock is near to each other, I lifted up my legs as he moves me back towards the wall as he lifts my legs up as he slides his cock into my pussy. as he holds my legs.

As I am against the wall of the shower as he pounds me, while the two of us are wet and the room is streamy as well as warm and moist as the two of us make love in our shower. While he pounded me, I had my arms around his neck as I close my eyes as he once more sucks on my neck and makes his way to my breast.

I could feel as he shoots his load inside of my pussy, as the two of us pant and breathe heavy as we recover from another round of sex. Soon afterwards, as the two of us helped each other wash up and then once we were done, the two of us get out of the shower, and headed to bedroom once more where we get dress.

Sighing I said, "You know I wanted to try that glory hole you know, but with all of what I did, I am not sure if I should do that at least not right now anyways."

"Well, you can just take your time, Aasta we don't want you to get sore from all of this sex, do we?" He said, as he asked me.

I smiled as I said, "Yes your right on that, anyways I guess I will wait a couple of days and see how I feel in a few days. Anyways so what are you planning for us to do today?"

"I thought we take a day off from scx, unless you wish to go out on your own if you wish." He answered me, as he laid back down on the bed.

I smiled as I said, "Yes your right we should have at least one or two days of rest, we don't want my little beautiful pussy to be too sore to have men fuck it."

He laughed as I then joined him on the bed, this time not naked, but dress. As the two of us then held each other as the two of us took a nap. However, the thoughts of me having more sexual adventures made me wonder what else is in store for me, and what other sexual mischief could I get myself into? Either way I need to rest and that way I will be prepared for another time and day

I soon fell asleep as with my husband, for now what could happen or will happen has to wait as the two of us, well mostly myself has had a long night last night at least for myself.

The End

Hotwife Aasta 1

Hello, my name is Aasta, and I consider myself as well as from others a hotwife, one which now has some experience under my belt so to speak, as such I am out looking for some adventure and fun, as it has been a week since I last had some sexual experiences.

However today I decided to go ahead and head to a park that I visited before and have some fun with the locals there, who I have had sex with beforehand, of course I will be wearing not that much, to make sure those who are looking to fuck women who are looking to be dogging at a park.

I am pretty sure that I will at least have three men there that will be more than willing to fuck me, as the three I have in mind have already fucked me beforehand. But I know there will be more than these three there, as I was told that this park is known for dogging, at least one of many that dogging happens.

Which makes me happy knowing there are other parks within the city that which I live in. So, as I gathered the few things that I needed to do what I want at the park, I than left in my car, as I headed to the park. Knowing full well that I could end up sore from what I am about to do, however I am fine with this.

Once I got to the park, I then parked my car in the main parking lot where I went to before. Once I got my things ready, I then opened the door as I did so I looked around and no one is around me, which only helps me be more into the mood as well as to let me know that what I have in mind will work. Well at least for now, unless I see more then what I expected to find here at this park.

I then stripped naked, and I took my necklace keyring as I had my keys, I then locked the door to my car as I headed down the pathway. Naked, and free from the confines of my clothes, I walked freely and without care in the world as to be honest the police have other concerns then to worry about people like myself or for others who look for people like myself.

As I walked, I enjoyed the freedom of being naked, and as I looked around, I smiled as I came across one of the men that fucked me before, he is over where I found him before. As he is sitting on a bench where the two of us had sex before, I came over to him and he looked up and smiled at me.

"I see you are back, once more and much bolder than I expected from you." He said, with a grin.

I then said to him with a smirk, "Well I am learning the trade of being a slut and a hotwife."

"Wait you are married?" he asked, me not in an angry or upset tone but more of a curious tone in his voice.

I answered him and said, "Yes I am married, is that an issue?"

"No, I just considered you not the type to be married, since you are a slut…hmm you were not always like this huh?" He asked me, as he started to fit the puzzle as he said with a snuff, as he smiled as he figured out my story.

I smiled as I said, "My husband knows that what I do, it was both our choice for this, lifestyle."

He nodded, as he asked, "Are you having fun with this newfound lifestyle that you have joined up with?"

"As much as I can, I do find myself wanting more then what I am able to have." I answered him, with a smirk.

He laughed as he said, "I bet anyways I take it you want me to fuck you again huh?"

"I won't mind if you still want to fuck me?" I asked him.

He grinned as he said, "Yes I do want to fuck you; however, I will tell you what we fuck here and then I take you to my place, and stay as you are, and once we are done, I will drop you off here or at your car."

Smiling I said to him, "That sounds good, I would love to head over to your place and then the two of us could have more time together. Also, I won't mind going with you naked, and back here again as that would be sexy."

"I am sure you and I will have a great time, as I can show you a good time, however you must also be willing to come to me often as I will always treat you with a special treat in a sexual way." He said with a grin, as he raised up and took down his pants.

I than moved over to the bench as I placed my hands on it as I leaned forth allowing him to use my expose ass and pussy. I smiled as I felt his hands touch my butt cheeks and then I felt his large cock enter my opening of my pussy as he slowly slides himself into me, as he did, he moaned as my pussy has not seen another cock other then my husband for a couple of days, so I am quite tight once more.

I started to moan as well, as he is for sure touching all the right places as he fucks me, as the two of us have sex again, as he fucks me, he spanks my ass, as he says to me, "Damn I kind of want to make you my own but you are already taken."

Smiling I then asked him, "I kind of want to have a baby from you, and I also won't mind having you, if you wish to become a lover?"

"Well, I won't mind helping you with the baby part, as for the lover part, well I know you will still be fucking other men, but sure." He answered me, as he continued fucking me.

As the two of us fuck out in the open in a park, at night. Both of us did not care if anyone sees us as we are, as part of the reason we are doing what we are doing is the thrill of being caught out here as we are having sex.

I then started to close my eyes as he is starting to make me moan a bit louder as he is for sure going to make me cum as well, soon I am moaning loud and I started to allow him to make me sing to him with my moans, as I did so it helped him wanting to fuck me harder to see what tones I can sing to him.

Now with my eyes closed and shut as I smiled as he started to pound my pussy as I could feel as an orgasm is on its way, as the orgasm hit, my singing changed which allowed him to even more so got excited as he pounded me faster and harder seeing how much of my singing can change even more.

As my orgasm ended, he then started to come as he started to pump his sperm into me as he did one powerful thrust into me as he stayed put, as he came deeply inside of my pussy. While this is happening, I am still very much moaning and making sure that my singing helps him with my moans.

After he fully came inside of me, and made sure he finished in me, he came out of me as he allowed me to get up and as he went away from me, as he got himself dress again, I raise up. The two of us smiled at each other, however I can sense that he has a surprise for me, other then himself having sex with me, however it doesn't matter as we both know that I am a slut after all.

Once the two of us were ready, he than had me follow him to his car, as once we got to his car, he opened up the door as he gave me a towel that he had to wipe myself with. As he opened the passenger door up, as I entered the car, still naked.

Then he entered the driver's seat as I shut the door, he didn't seem to mind or care that I am naked in the car as he started to car as the two of us headed to his place, there I am sure I will once more have some good times with him.

Since I don't have to check in with my husband, and he of course is fine with what I do and how I do things, I have as much time with this man as I want to have. As the two of us then got to his place, as I saw he lives in a nice house with a large yard and even a better yard in the back from what I can tell.

The two of us get out of the car, as I followed him to the door, as he unlocks the door as the two of us enter the house together. Both him and I later on have sex and not only with him but with other surprises that he had in store for me, I stay at his house for a couple of weeks with him as my body is made to feel great pleasure and the fact that my mind has opened up to new forms of sex that I never image I could ever experience before.

When I return home my husband is amaze at the newfound sexual freedom and experience that I have learned and as such is impress with my new friends. However, what happen is for another story and another time.

The End

Abagail Aslam Starts a Family of Three

A couple of days ago, someone I still love and I someone I would have married instead of my husband Jason, came back into my life again, his name is John. The three of us had a threesome, and at that at least Jason said I became a hotwife as a sexual thing.

The issue I take with that I am no slut or a whore, I rather have both of them or none at all, I am legality married to Jason, and as such John came back to town after his tour in the service was over.

Like I said, if John never left to go into the service, four years ago, I would have been his wife and no one else in my life would be at the same point that both of them are at. Its hard to explain but both of them I have the same feelings towards. They both complete me, take away one and I feel like a part of me is missing.

I need both of them and they both know and understand that, I don't want to be a "hotwife" to others I want to be a hotwife to both of them, if I was to become a slut or a whore I want to be their slut and whore not to anyone else. Because if I was to be put into a situation where I am with other men, I am sorry I won't be able to do anything other than a open hole and empty shell.

I am not saying they would be raping me no, I am saying I would have no feelings for the other men, as such I would be more of a emotionless woman, while her body is having sex with men she doesn't know. Now take it to where both John and Jason are there but that is all that is there and there many copies of them, yes I would be into it hardcore, as they do me. But that is not the way things work in real life.

Since the threesome that, my husband Jason, John and I were in John has stayed with us as I told my husband I want him to stay here for awhile and he agreed. Later on in the day, we will have a talk as I want to talk to both of them about what I wanted to do.

In short I want to have the two of them share me, and I become a shared wife as the two of them are my husband's and not have a legality married husband and a lover, but a legality married husband and a spiritual husband.

So as I prepared myself to talk with the two of them about this, I sighed as I drink my morning coffee, as John is still here but Jason had to work well he works from the morning to mid afternoon as he has a average 9 to 5 job as they are called but he is more than the average grunt so to speak at his job.

John than comes into the room, as he has his own room, he is wearing just some boxers and a shirt and he smiles when he sees me, and he asked, "Can I have some of that coffee you made?"

"Sure John I make it for all of us to be honest." I answered him with a smile.

He than got out a cup and he poured himself some as he placed sweeter and some milk into it and than he started to drink it, he than said to me, "Damn this is good coffee, Abagail."

"Thank you." I said with a blush and a smile.

He than said with a sigh, "I hope I wasn't rough with you the other day when me and your husband did you while you were asleep."

I took a deep breathe and said, "You both felt good as the two of you had sex with me, which is why I need to talk to the two of you later on."

"Oh so this has nothing to do with how I did things with you I take it?" He asked me.

I shocked my head and I said, "It has to do with our future, and how I want things."

I than started to leave the kitchen as I have already had my first cup, he nodded his head as I assume he could tell what I am talking about. After a bit I went into the living room and sat down for a bit as I started to read a book.
The rest of the day was pretty unimportant both John and I talked about things but nothing sexual as I wanted to wait till at least Jason is home, not that I didn't want to have sex with John or Jason by themselves I wanted to talk a bit more about things first.

After Jason got home, I waited for him to get unwind from being from work mode to home mode, after a bit I had both of them in the living room, as I sat down they sat down across from me as I sat on the couch and they were on two of the chairs in there.

I than started by saying, "I wanted to have this talk because of what happen two days ago, and I have decided more about what I would like and what I feel would be the best for all of us as a family."

"The fact is this, I love the both of you, and if one is gone I will feel a part of me is also gone, so I would like it if both of you stay and become my husband's." I said, with a smile.

Jason asked, "I kind of figured you may have something like this planned which is fine but what about if John gets you pregnant?"

"Easy we will make it known that John is here as a spiritual husband, no legal things at all, and the two of you can work, John doesn't have work right now but I am sure he will at some point." I answered as I smiled at both.

John asked, "So what about jealously between the two of us, I mean how are you going to handle the two of us?"

"I want the two of you sleeping with me, if that means I have threesomes every time I have sex than I don't mind, also the fact is this, the two of you have to be ok with making love to me at the same time, not by yourselves." I said, as I thought about this a bit, more as I really liked the both of them having sex with me than to have one at a time.

I than added, "When it comes to sex the two of decided where you have sex in me at that time, I have no issues with any of my holes being done by either one of you, but this is the thing I don't want any of you being upset at the other if the other gets me pregnant. I want to be a mother and I want to have children with the both of you, I want you two to be their fathers and doesn't matter which one of you got me pregnant, the two of you by having sex with me, is sharing with me your genetics as such in my mind the child or children are the both of yours."

Jason than asked me, "So what if we want to have another wife would you be against that?"

Hmm, something I was not expecting from either of them, to ask. I than sighed as I closed my eyes, as I answered Jason, "Ok since you are sharing me than fine I will share the two of you with others, however I am the head wife. Is that fair,?"

They both nodded as John asked, "Besides the two of us will there be any other husbands you want?"

"I am not a slut or a whore, too strangers, I will be for the two of you, I will be your hotwife but to no one else." I said as I had my eyes opened again, as I said with a straight face, as I said, "So no one else for another husband. Just the two of you."

They both laughed and Jason said, "Well I guess that is a good thing."

I than asked them point blank, "Do you two agree with this or are you against my idea?"

"I am ok with it as I can see without John you will be hurt which is why I invited him here and why I was ok with the threesome in the first place." Jason said, as he had a smile of approval on his face.

John said, "I am fine with it, as long as the two of you are ok with it, and yes I do still have a lot of feelings for you Abagail."

"So what about last names Abagail?" Jason asked, as he asked again, "So who are you going to have as your last name me or John's last name?"

"I am married to you Jason legality which is why my last name is Aslam." I answered Jason as I added, "For children before we go there, we will have them be both of your last names included that way the children will know that they are part of a larger family."

Jason than asked, "What about other wives we both decided to take it will be like the same issue with between me and John or would they take upon the last name of their mother?"

"I guess it would be their mother but I am not sure as I am still new to this, also I am doing this because I need the both of you I can't do with one one or the other." I answered to the best way I can.

They already knew this and than John sighed as did Jason, the two looked at each other and smiled as Jason said, "I am ok with this, however John at some point will need to work and help out in some way or another."

"I also agree but I am not going to look for another wife, however if Jason wants one he is free to do so, but the question is will he share her or would I need one for myself, but either way this sounds very good for me." He said, as he added, "Also I don't really have anyone else that I would want to be with besides you Abagail. So this all works well for me, and don't worry I am sure something will come up work wise for me."

I smiled as I than said, "Well here is the thing we all have had sex together so that doesn't need to be done, to make this official but anyways I want the two of you not just for the sex, but also I need the two of you."

They nodded at me as they both smirk at me, I than smiled and blush as now I have two husbands something most women would maybe think about as a fantasy but I have it for real, now the three of us have to come up with plans for the future like how or where everyone fits into the larger puzzle of a family.

The three of us than planned for different things, as John said this, "One thing I would say for us as a family we should plan not just for children and the sexual side of things but also for defending ourselves and preparing for anything that could happen, I seen a lot of things and heard a lot of things within the military to know it is a good idea to be prepared for anything and everything the best we can."

"I have to agree with that one as well." Jason also said, as he kind of looked a bit worried.

I nodded as the three of us talked some more, and a plan of action for our family started to take shape, such as the cost of food, and everything else that we all need and want. The other things such as the cost of gas, as well as for tools and other things were added.

So far everything is doable with the job that Jason has however, with John's help once he starts to work it would increase many times more our ability to support each other, as I do not work however I have some ideas that could help with bringing more cash into our family.

Later on as most of the planning has started to take effect, and we were all back at home, the three of us prepare for bed, as in to have sex well more importantly to make love. Although to do this, again since we have all agreed that we will become a family all three of us, as both Jason and John will both share me as their wife.

We all agreed that the best way to do things is for me to be naked and no lingerie at least not yet. As the two men who are my husband's laid on the bed naked I took off my clothes in front of them as I only had clothes that I wear when going to bed.

Now in the nude I went onto the bed and I smiled as I went between each of them as I started to slowly stroke one of them as I started to have oral with the other, as his cock went into my mouth I had full control of how I wanted things, as they laid there as they allowed me to do the work myself.

As I switch from one man to the other as I wanted the both of them to be as erected as possible, after this was done, I than picked who I wanted to be on top of, once I picked that man, which in this case was Jason, I went on top of his cock slowly as I helped guide him into me as he was in me all the way I than started to bounce on him as I took hold of my breast as John went in back me to help me with my breast as he sucked on my neck as I rode on Jason.

After a while I than felt as he inserted his cock into my ass, which made me lean more towards Jason as I put my hands firmly on the bed to keep me from going completely onto Jason.

Closing my eyes as John slowly slides his cock in and out of my ass, while I am still bouncing on Jason, after awhile he started to thrust into me with the aid of my own movement we went in deeper into me, after awhile I started to grow tired and I laid down onto Jason as he than wrapped his hands around me as he held me in place as both men fucked me.

As I was moaning though out this whole thing, my moans started to grow louder as I cried out as I could feel an orgasm coming as both men buried their cocks deeper into me, "Oh God yes keep fucking me, I am about to come!"

After that the two men went even faster as I started to orgasm I closed my eyes as Jason kisses and sucked on my neck which made my emotions go even more wilded as my orgasm made my body shake and tumble as the two of them started to come deep inside both holes, at that moment I knew who will be the father of the first of our children it will be Jason.

Too be honest I didn't plan on getting pregnant at all, with this I wanted to just relax and allow my two husbands to make love to me, not to get me pregnant well, at least not yet. I am not saying this child will be unwelcome no in fact he or she will be very welcome, and in fact very loved.

After John finished inside of me, he gently laid down on me as he kissed my back of my neck as Jason was spasming in me as he finish coming inside of my vagina, after a bit John rolled over as Jason moved me to make me become a sandwich as both men were on either sides of me, as Jason is still deep inside of me, I could feel as John's cock is still very large and I helped him put himself back in my ass.

It didn't take long before I fell asleep with the two of them in me, as we all fell asleep naked once more. I am going to love having two husbands, instead of having one.

After a couple of weeks, I did get a pregnancy test to see if I am pregnant or not and the results came back positive, I knew from the moment that both Jason and John was having sex with me every night since we became one family that I would become pregnant.

As after the time we made it official that both Jason and John will share me we have had a threesome every night, and I for sure been loving it, as one of them is in either my ass or my pussy.

Once I found that I am indeed pregnant I than went to the doctor and yes it is confirmed that I am indeed pregnant, so I came home and let them know. They were both happy, but John seemed a bit worried or concern I should say, he seems happy but something seems to be bothering him.

For now I will let him come to me, and I feel it has nothing to do with me, or the baby, but something else. Like something that had to do with maybe something he knows not sure. For now like I said I will let him tell me when he is ready.

However the good thing is now we will have a child on the way, and to be honest other than whatever is upsetting John, the good news for him is he now has a job as well. So everything seems to be falling into place nicely for us.

As both Jason and John prepare a room for our child, I learned that I am having a daughter, from everything I believe Jason to be the father, which works fine, as no one knows that John is also my husband as in spiritual one.

Like before I have noticed that John has been paying a lot of his funds for building a fallout shelter for us and stocking it well with things, Jason has not said anything but he seems to be on John's side on this matter.

The two of them have been working on this project and keeping things away from me, not because there is something going on but almost as if they don't want the scare me, also there has been a lot of tense in the air, and I don't mean with my husbands and me, but in general.

I am hearing a lot of reports of some sort of conflict coming up, and maybe John knows something I don't however I am not going to worry about it right now, as things seem to still be normal other than a tension in the air, as if people are concern or worried about this conflict that could happen.

However I can't control what I can't control so why should I worry for now, anyways right now I am more concern with our child and to know that we will have a daughter is another thing to be happy about.

For now, I will focus on now and not than, I have nothing against my husband's preparing for whatever as to me that is what they are here for as I will just do what I know I need to do, and that is to make sure that our daughter will grow up and be loved by her two father's.

The End

Abagail Aslam The Hotwife

One day I came home from work, and my husband is waiting in the front room for me, as I came into the house I than smiled at him as I place my things down that I had in the front room, so that it is easy for us to not forget when we go anywhere.

I asked him, "Honey have you been waiting for me, to come home all this time and whats going on?"

"Well Abagail I have an idea if you wish to try it out that is?" He asked me

I than asked him, "Ah so what will that be?"

"Well we have talked about this before and I was hoping maybe you have thought about this some more as in the two of us having a threesome with another man involved." He answered me, as I took a deep breathe.

I than said, "Yes I remember us talking about this before but the issue I have is this that I want to only have a child with you and no one else."

"Yes I know but he could do your ass or mouth as I only do your pussy." He said, as to try to help me out with the decision.

I sighed as I asked, "Fine but do you have someone already lined up for this, or have you not even started to look yet?"

"Oh I have someone already in mind, and he will be coming over in an hour or so." He said, as I sighed and rolled my eyes back as he already started things even if he was not sure if I was wanting to do this or not.

I sighed again as I smirk, "Well looks like you lucked out, fine I will do this, and try it out, but after this make sure I am ok with it first, I am not saying I disapprove but lets do this as a couple and not go ahead and make plans without letting me know first."

"Well I am already for it, do you want to shower before he gets here?" He asked, as he nodded before letting me know he understood what I meant.

I than said, "Yes I will be getting myself cleaned up in a bit, I will just have a towel over myself when I am done with my shower so I won't waste time in getting dress only to get naked once more."

He nodded as I went to get undress in the bathroom and to take my shower, as I showered I washed myself up as much as I could and I made myself smell nice so he wouldn't have any issues with the way I smell or appear, since I did just come home from work. One thing on his side is I was planning to shower anyways.

After I was done, I dried up and put the towel around my body and I head out of the bathroom as I held onto the dirty clothes and I placed them in a dirty clothes bin we have setup for us. Also since we do plan on have children at some point we have a child's room setup even with a crib, I am not pregnant yet but we have talked about things to excite our sex life a bit to maybe help me release an egg, this was one idea as in adding another person into the mix as we have sex.

I than went into our room, and I dropped the towel to the ground as I shut the door, I went to lay down as I wait for them both, now completely naked its just the waiting game, as I wait I wonder who it maybe or if I knew them.

After a bit, the door opens and my husband and a good friend of my came into the room, one that I knew had feelings for me at one time. He blush as he saw me nude for the first time, I see my husband brought someone over that yes I won't be afraid to see me naked as well as to have sex with.

See this friend his name is Jason, I have liked but my husband John well we well I got married to him, not because we had too I married him, because Jason had to go away as he joined the military for awhile, now I see he is back in town.

Jason said to me, "Well not sure what to say about all of this Abagail I didn't think I would see you again, and expressly seeing you nude and also about to have a threesome with you and John."

"Well I rather you had sex with me than someone else I don't know all that much, I change my mind John Jason can come inside of my pussy if he wishes too." I said, and John smirk.

He said, as in John, "I kind of thought so, but its all good."

As the two of them got naked in front of me, and than I got up and went over to the both of them as I kneel down and I started to suck on Jason's sock first, I have never had sex with Jason, only my husband have I had sex with. Even oral or anal has only been with John.

As I stroke my husband's cock as I took Jason's cock into my mouth which is about the same size, and width as my husbands, so this will be fun for sure. I than started to moan as he went forth down my throat as I closed my eyes as I went from one man to the next.

After a bit I than stopped before either one of them ended up coming in my mouth or on my hand, which would end things too quick for things to truly begin. I than stood up as than Jason as well as my husband stood up and I than took Jason's hand and I than had him go to the foot of the bed and I gently motion onto him to fall down, he did so and laid on the pillows, I than went on the bed as I went over him and as I did I lower myself onto his cock, as his penis slowly slided into me I closed my eyes as I moaned as his cock is than firmly inside of me I than laid down on him as I prepared my ass to have my husband fuck me.

I allowed him to chose if he wanted to fuck my ass or join with Jason as the two fuck my pussy together. After a bit he went onto the bed as I waited to feel his cock either in my ass or pussy my body grow excited as I have never experience two men in me at once even with a dildo I than started to kiss Jason on his forehead as he started to neck me and sucked on my thin neck.

As he did that I moaned even louder as I felt my husband preparing himself to enter me, I than felt his cock enter my ass, as he did rolled my eyes back and said with a cry of pleasure, "Oh my God this feels fucking good yes fuck me the two of you!"

After I said that the two of them started to thrust in and out of both holes, as I knew at some point as we are doing this both of my holes will have sperm deep inside of them, I grew even more turned on and excited as to the thought of sperm in my ass at the same time someone else's cum in my pussy.

Jason put his arms around me as he had a hand by my ass as John my husband slammed into my ass, I rolled my eyes back as the two of them started to go deeper and faster into me.

I orgasm as I yelled in a cry of passion, "Oh God I am coming!"

After which the two of them increase their speed and fucked me harder at the same time, wanting to put their warm seed into me, after awhile I felt as I started to calm down from the orgasm as I moan softly as I had the two of them fucking me deeply, as they both fucked me hard and fast.

I than felt as they both filled me up as they both took my holes, panting and moaning as the feelings and emotions I had were nothing like I had before, I didn't really wish for this to stop.

I have became a hotwife, however I truly am not totality sure if I want anyone else other than my husband and Jason, yet. As I am enjoying how much these two men of my are giving me pleasure, the other thing is to submit myself to strangers is one thing but having sex with friends and people I know is another.

The truth here is yes I had sex just now and a threesome but they made love to me, and not just to fuck me, they cared how I felt, strangers on the other hand would care about themselves, however the issue now is if I truly don't want how I am feeling to end than I will have to have more than two men having sex with me.

As I still bask in the afterglow of having sex with two men whom I have feelings for and in many ways would love to have both as spouses, the fact is I am starting to wonder how more would bring me.

I am not done with this, as the two men who are still deeply inside of me, touch and kiss my naked flesh as I soon got to relax to care if they start up again or not, I soon fell asleep as I felt once more as I grin they started to once more fuck me. Smiling as I felt them having sex with me again, my dream of not ever having this end won't come true in the sense of them but could with the sense of others.

I than doze off to sleep land as they were still having sex with me, I didn't mind or cared as they were rocking me like a baby I soon fell asleep in their warm, loving grasp…

The End

Acca the Hotwife Tied Up Threesome

My name is Acca Caswell and my husband is going to share me tonight, as he is having one of his friends come over tonight as my husband and his friend both have sex with me, however I will be tied up as I am having sex. So like every time my husband and I make love I am getting ready to take a shower, as I did so my husband prepares the bed for me so that once I am done with my shower all I will need to do is just dry off and then lay on the bed as he ties me to the bed.

I told him I am ok, with have oral and vaginal but no anal, at least not as I am tied up. Also not yet, I may change my mind later on as I got use to having sex being tied up this way. This way I will be well prepared for myself being tied as I have other men touch me as well as enter me at the same time. So as I shower and make sure that my body smells good, as well as clean up from the days actives that I did during the course of the day.

Making sure that I am as clean as I can be, I then stop the water as I step outside of the tub and I reach for the towel that is waiting for me. As I started to dry myself off as well as I can, as I will be laying down on the bed naked without any clothes. Of course this has happened many times before when my husband and I have sex. However tonight is different as I will have someone else seeing me naked as well as having sex with me at the same time.

The other issue at hand is this, as I am nervous but at the same time I am willing to try this as my husband will be there with me, as well as having sex with me at the same time. However there is one minor detail that I have yet said, the fact that both my husband and I are Mormons as such we would have never thought of doing this a few months ago. However the other fact is this, we have a hard time believing in the Mormon Church and as such we are trying something that we have never done before.

See we have been married now for two years and as such we have not yet been able to have a child, we have both gotten check out and we should be able to have a baby. So my husband started to look into other means these means did not work as well, then him and I started to talk about maybe I should try having another man's sperm in me. At first my husband was a bit upset with the idea, then he countered my offer by asking me if I would be ok with having another man have sex with me, as he does me as well.

I at first did not like the idea but then he told me if I was ok with having another man's sperm inside of me, why would I have an issue of having another man have sex with me. We both then talked about it more and then we decided well the Church at one time practice polygamy however that is with having one husband and that husband having many wives. What we talked about is different in fact it will be where I will have many husbands and my husband has one wife or maybe we both will have more then one spouse.

So after we both talked about this some more, my husband talked to a friend of his who knows me and I know him. He is not a member and has always had an interest in me, but never told me before. He is not married and as such, my husband talked to him and so now tonight is the night the three of us have some fun.

I would be lying if I said I am not afraid, the truth is I am scared of this but at the same time I want to try it out. As this will be my first time with another man other then my husband. To be honest I do not feel I am sinning as my husband is in the room with me, and he will be having sex with me as well. However I wonder if maybe by doing this with both my husband and our friend that I have a child, that the child could be in fact from my husband. The fact that we are married it won't draw any questions if I get pregnant as that is what the Church wants is for a married couple to have children.

They don't need to know that I had an extra man involved with helping me get pregnant. Either way I am almost done drying off, as I then took the towel I used as I went into the bedroom, there my husband is waiting for me, he is still dress as it will be easy for him to answer the door being dress then to be naked. I gave him the towel and he folded it in half as he put it on the bed. As he did so it will act as a guide for me to lay on top of, that way I will know where and to lay on top of.

He then said, "Ok Acca now it is time, so get onto the bed and get as comfortable as you can."

I nodded as I got onto the bed as I did so I got myself as comfortable as I can, I then said, "Ok I am ready."

After I said that he then started to tie my hands and feet to the bed, he did it in a tight secure way but not too tight that it could hurt me, or cause harm. He also made it easy for him to untie me once he is done. After he was done, he then smiled as he left me in the bedroom now tied to the bed and naked. The whole reason I am tied in the first place is that it was our friends idea, as I guess he has this fetish of this sort of thing.

Laying there naked and expose to whomever or whatever my husband brings into the room. This is more about trust and not about control of my body, as I trust my husband not to leave me here and then bring to me men who I did not know, or want to have sex with me. As I am now at his mercy and as such I am at his disposal to do with as he please however I know he won't do anything at least now to betray my trust with him.

The only thing I can do is lay there on our bed, waiting for both my husband and our friend to come into the room. I just look around as I can't do anything other then wait for the two of them to come into the bedroom, and then for them to get naked. Then the two of them can use my body whatever way they want, other then having my butt done, as I don't want to have anal sex yet.

However, I am willing for them to use my mouth, as my husband and I have had oral sex before. But that is not what I am concern with, I am concern with what if we are found out, that my husband and I have another man in the mix. I sighed to myself, as I heard the door open and the my husband and our friend started to talk.

Now it is too, late as I will have my husband and our friend have sex with me. I guess I will have to allow this to happen, hmm that didn't sound right as I am allowing this to happen I could have many times tell my husband no I am not interested in this, but now I am far past the point of no return as I hear them coming towards the bedroom.

My heart is pounding as I keep my eyes on the door way to the hall, as I now noticed that my husband shut the door, and as such I have no idea when they will come. I then heard as the door knob is opening my body is starting to grow from fear to excitement and my vagina is starting to betray me as my body knows that soon another man will enter me.

After waiting for awhile the door opens up and my husband lets our friend in and he sees me. He grins at me, as I smile at him, as he scans my nakedness as well as the fact I am tied to the bed, waiting for him to fuck me. My body is betraying me, as I watch as the two men get naked, as they did so our friend is first to be naked, as I see his already erected cock, I think to myself "Oh my God he is larger then my husband he will stretch me out more then my husband has!"

As I gasp at the size of his cock, he then starts to come towards me and as he does he touches my body and then he gets onto the bed as he does so I start to shock as my body knows that I will soon have this giant cock inside of me. I am starting to find myself not afraid of it, but rather wanting it deep inside of me, I want him to fuck me with it as my desires have taken over.

Coming over to me he then gets himself at my pussy with his mouth as I realizes he is going to eat me out first before he starts to fuck me. Wrapping his arms around both my legs as he positions me as much as I can being tied up as he starts to bury his tongue inside of my pussy as I gasp with pleasure as his tongue and the way he is doing it makes it feel like there is a cock inside of me.

He starts to fuck me with his tongue, as he goes down deeper inside of my vagina I start to moan as I started to moan I then felt as a head of a cock is tapping against my cheek. I turn into that direction like a child who is still sucking on his or her mother does as the child finds the breast. As I turn I see my husband's cock waiting for me, I open my mouth wide to take his cock inside of my mouth.

As my husband slides his cock deep down my throat I close my eyes as I am being eaten out and having my husband fuck my mouth. After a bit my husband starts to thrust his cock deeper down my throat as he knows I can take it deep, as he has many times in the past, he also knows I love oral above anything else.

Doing that he rubs my hair as if I was a pet and he says in a sexual tone, "Babe want to have my cock in your mouth as he fucks you?"

I couldn't reply other then to make grunts as to say yes, as his cock slide up and down my throat. With each thrust down my throat I would make a gaggling sound which someone would say my husband is hurting me but in fact no I am not being hurt as it makes me more turned on hearing myself make that sound, at the same time oral sex feels good for me.

After awhile our friend stopped eating me out as now I am nice and wet as well as ready for him to enter me. Knowing full well what is about to happen soon as my mouth is being fucked, I started to get more excited knowing soon our friend's large dick will enter me and fill me up as well as more then likely tear me a bit more. I am not looking for the tearing up of my pussy a bit more, but I am looking for the pleasure that he will of course give to me. As he prepared me for him my excitement grow more and more, as my fear of all of this is now gone.

I still have my eyes close as my husband is inside my mouth, which I think also helps with the fear of what is about to happen to my poor pussy. Too be fair my pussy is not poor as it will soon have a choice cock enter it and give not only myself pleasure but it as well, perhaps even so much pleasure that he will make me a mother and him a father. However the father will be my husband even if he is the one who made me pregnant.

Feeling the tip of his head of his penis at the opening of my vagina as he slowly press it inside of me, as he slowly entered me I got more and more excited and turned on as he started to fill me up. I have to say he does fill me up and so far I feel no pain, other then pressure from the size of him, he is giving me his cock in a very loving and slow way so my body can get use to the size and so it does not hurt. He knows that he is the 2nd man inside of me, and as such I never had a man inside of me his size before.

After a while he is completely inside of me, as he then slowly slides his penis in and out of me. Although he is thrusting in me, he is not doing so very fast yet, as he wants me to get use to his size. As he did so and with my husband fucking my mouth I am moaning as well as I can as he is starting to pound my mouth.

This is the first time I have two men inside of me at the same time, and to boot the first time I am tied up as I am having sex. As both men slide their members inside of me, the closer it will become where the two of them will fill me up with their sperm, however my husband will be more then likely the first to come inside of me. As I think about it more, the idea of his sperm spilling down my throat and inside of my stomach excites me, as I also know that our friend once he comes inside of me I have a feeling with the amount of pleasure I am having, I hate to say this but I will release an egg.

See that has been the issue for me, timing or the fact that my husband did not excite me enough so that an egg would release. Well with what is happening now I am for sure going to release one. Also yes I have had orgasms before with my husband, however they were mild compared to what I can sense with the one coming to me soon.

My husband then said, "I am about to come Babe I love you and I know you love it when I do this to you."

As he said that my stomach got excited knowing his seed is about to come to it, and become part of my body, which as I thought that I started to have the orgasm, as it started he started to come as I could taste and feel him as he thrust as deep into my throat as he can as he filled my stomach up with his cum. As he spray his seed inside my throat he made sure every drop was in me, as he slowly slide his cock out of my mouth. As he did so I swallowed whatever was left as his cock left my mouth.

I am still be pounded in my pussy as I opened up my eyes and smiled at my husband as he smiled at me as he took one of my tied up hands as the two of us embrace as he started to kiss my mouth as he locked in a French kiss as my body is being rocked back and forth with another cock still inside of me. I am also having an orgasm, which so far I can contain but it is a large one, which is a good sign to say the less.

Kissing as our friend is fucking me, which I am sure is helping him as he watches the two of us kiss as he fucks me. Moaning with each thrust deep inside of me, as my husband and I kiss as his tongue is in me where his cock once was. I then started to orgasm harder as I felt a bit weird inside of me where my womb is at.

My body then arch up towards our friend so he can fuck me harder and deeper as my body knows that I am about to release an egg and he will be the father. Even while tied up I am able to do so, as this happens he goes down deeper inside of me, making it for sure that his seed will impregnate me. He knew off the bat that we wanted children and the whole reason other then to have more pleasure and fun is for me to have a child, so he of course acted in kind helping me become a mother.

He then said, "Acca I am coming now."

After he said that he then went as deep inside of me as he could, as he grunted and moan as he started to fill my womb up with his seed at the same time, I know I just release an egg. There is no way, I won't be able to conceive as he is filling my womb up as my husband and I then started to kiss more and his tongue goes deeper inside of me.

When he is done coming in me he then slowly exited my pussy as my husband then raise up as the two of us stopped kissing. Our friend got off the bed as I can hear him panting as he as well as me orgasm. He then went over to his clothes and started to get dress as my husband then got off the bed as well leaving me there. I have a feeling he has more planned for me, maybe he wants his turn as well.

As the two of them get dress and then they left me in the room again by myself with no one but myself in here still tied to the bed and still naked. However this time, I have cum dripping down from my vagina. I have to say in a lot of ways I enjoyed what happened to me just now, and I think I will enjoy having our friend have sex with me with my husband, however if I am indeed pregnant I am also not against having more men do me as well now that I am a bit used to it now.

I could hear as the door opened up and closed as I could tell our friend left, I kind of was sadden as I wanted him to stay a bit longer then he did. Maybe even stay the night as he ravage my body as I am tied to the bed, but oh well. I then heard as my husband is coming towards the door as he opens up he has a grin on his face and he comes inside the room.

He shuts the door as he said, "He really enjoyed having sex with you, he does hope he got you pregnant but he also is wanting to have sex with you more often."

"That is fine with me, I like the way he did me." I said to my husband.

He then started to take off his clothes again, and he said, "Oh he will be back but right now, you have been naughty by having sex with someone other then me."

I know he is just role playing a bit as I said with a smile, "If I been naughty then take my ass as I been a bad little girl and I have became a slut. Do you want me to become your slut?"

"Yes I do Acca." He said as he came closer to me.

His cock is getting harder as he came onto the bed as he had some lube with him. This will be my first time having anyone in my ass, but I figured why now. Now is the time, if I am going down the path of being a hotwife I may as well have all holes done. However I want my husband to take my ass first and not anyone else, as he took my pussy and mouth first before anyone else. So it is only fair for him to take my ass.

As he got himself ready as he is between my legs he got himself as large as he can get as he then put lube in my ass, which started to get excited and my pussy started to get horny again. Then he entered my ass as he slowly went inside of me seeing if I can handle it or not, so far it felt good. Then he slided it in me as far into me as he can take it, as he went on top of me, as the two of us started to kiss as he fucked my ass like a pussy.

Moaning he then stopped kissing me as he started to neck me as my body rocked back and forth as with each thrust he rocked me back. As he mark me up with his mouth and tongue as I am moaning and crying out in passion, telling him to fuck me harder and faster. This excited him more so as then he couldn't take it anymore as he started to come in me.

He stayed inside of me for a bit longer as then he went out of me, as he then rolled over on the other side of me. I am still here tied up as he is on my side, as he recovered from doing my ass he gently touch my breast as he lean forward and started to suck on one of them, as he did so he started to untie me. After a bit he completely untied me from my bonds.

Now free we are now too tired to care if we are naked and as such we held each other as we both go to sleep. As I start to doze off I smile as I can feel the cum from both of them still inside of me.

The End

Agurtzane Becomes A Hotwife

Hello, my name is Agurtzane, as my husband and I have talked about maybe making things for ourselves more sexual, and to expand our sex life, we have both decided to have me go out and become a hotwife or a shared wife of sorts. However, I will need to tell my husband everything that has happened with each time I have any sexual encounters.

So, I decided to go ahead and find somewhere to experiment at, and I have a couple of ideas of where to go, one will be somewhere that I have heard a lot about, such as at a adult bookstore, or other words called a arcade, the others will be at a adult theater and of course at a adult sex club, or other words known as a swingers club.

My point is I want to go to every single place at least once and maybe go back to each one more then one time, depending on how I like it or not. However, for today I am planning to head over to an adult bookstore, not just to have sex but to also check to see what else they have in order for me to get ideas.

Once I get there, I will check things out more so, and maybe plan for another place or I may stay there and explore more. So, as I get ready to head out, as I headed out, my husband wave good bye as he knows that I am going to be exploring my sexual side of myself.

I then took what I needed to have, and I dress up in a slutty outfit that I could find that is in my wardrove and I left our home as we don't want to yet have any action at our home just yet anyways. This could change however for now the plan is for me to have all the sexual adventures outside the home.

As I got myself ready as in, I made sure I had everything on me that I will need, I then left our home, and I headed to my car. Once I was in my car I then took off to where I feel would be the best choice which happens to be an adult bookstore like I said. Although I am planning to not only try to see where a good place to have sex with random men there, I also want to get some ideas in terms of watch porn there, as well as see if they have any sexual aids so that I could enjoy sex much better as well as the men who have sex with me as well.

Once I got to the adult bookstore, the sign of the name of the place and a medium size parking lot, as I drove into the lot, and parked my car I then got out of the car as I did, I made sure I had my keys and my purse.

Once I was completely out of the car and after I have locked up my vehicle I then headed inside of the place, as I entered the shop the place looked like any other retail shops but with one major change everything is about sex.

At the counter there is a young woman who is the clerk, she is maybe 18 or 19 not sure but for sure a young person compared to me whom is nearly 30 years old. I came up to her as she watched me come into the place, as she seemed to not be concern of me being there, as I came up, I showed her my ID saying that I am old enough to be here. She smiled as she then went back doing what she was doing which as I got closer, I saw she was reading a book.

Nearing closer I saw that the book was about history, she then saw that I was coming near her as to either ask a question or to buy something. She then looked up at me, and smiled as she asked, "Can I help you?"

"Yes, I was wondering as this is my first time here or for that matter at an adult bookstore, I was wondering about what you have here?" I asked in a voice that is not nervous or not scared, but with a voice that is calm and knows what I want.

She then answered me, in a polite and friendly way, "Well that is why I am here to help you out, but first I need to know what it is you are looking for or are interested in as there are things here that can be well more for those who are seeking some sexual fun now, or if you're looking for a product?"

"Well, both, I am new at this hotwife sort of thing, and would like to find more interesting toys, clothes, and of course sex now." I said, as I answered her.

She then grin as if she has seen people like myself before, and she then came to the other side of the counter and she said, "I have seen others who are interested in becoming a good hotwife or shared wife for their husbands and boyfriends before, so you have come to the right place, I also can see that you are not scared about this or nervous which I see a lot in new comers to this sort of life style."

"Anyways come follow me, I will show you somethings." She said as she led me around the store.

While she did so I saw the many products and videos that would be good for me to view either by myself or with my husband. Also, she showed me lubes, condoms, and lingerie that I could have while having sex with my husband and others, or others. Some of the lingerie looks very sexual and would make me stand out more so.

I then asked her, "So I have heard about a glory hole do you have them here?"

"Yes, we do in our arcade area and our viewing rooms, not all rooms have them, but we do have them here, as well as private rooms, which can be used for a husband and wife or friends, as well as a play area that one can have a bit more fun in." She said, as she answered me.

I smiled as I asked her, "Hmm, would you think it would be ok if I would try out one of the gloryholes?"

"I think if you feel as if you are ready to try one of the rooms with a glory hole inside of it, then there is no reason to stop you from it, I would say that if you want to know when the men come over to do their things to the women or men that use the gloryhole I can tell you, which will give you much more time to experiment with the gloryhole and at the same time have enough men to have sex with you." She said to me, as she seemed to be very helpful.

I then said to her, "Sure I would like to know what timeframe to come for the most action."

She smiled as she said, "I kind of thought you would say that, here follow me back to the counter."

The two of us then went back to the counter, and since it is still pretty slow with customers etc., she then got out a pad of paper and a pen as she then wrote down the times when it is the busiest. After that she handed me the piece of paper, and I took it and I looked at it as I did so I smiled as I have a bit of time before the fun starts.

I then thank her, as I went into the store to get a couple of things which caught my eye mainly some lingerie that will make me much more sexual looking then what I have on not, however what I am getting is not all for here but is for other places as well.

After I have gotten what I wanted, I then headed over to the clerk and she rang them up and I paid for them, after a bit I left the store with my new collection of lingerie, lubes as well as some porn videos for me to look at later on. However, I want to head back home for a bit to prepare for what I will be doing later on at the adult bookstore.

Once I got to my car, I opened my car up and I placed my things on the passenger side of the car, and I then took off, my goal is to head back home for a bit like I said and prepare for things in a couple of hours.

Once I got home, I got my things into our home and I went to the master bedroom, as I went to our room, my husband did not say anything as he knew I won't be having any action this soon and knew me well enough to know that I would have told him what has happened if anything did.

I made it to our bedroom, with all the things I got today, and I placed all the lingerie into a drawer, that I had that was empty. After I got everything put away, I then started to get myself undress and this time I put on one of the lingerie and I then put on some pants which looked like I was wearing regular clothes but in fact I was wearing mostly a lingerie and some pants.

After I was done, I got myself ready and I also added lube and a hand towel to my things as well as some other personal items to help clean myself after everything is said and done. Once I got everything, I needed prepped and ready to go, I then once more left my home and headed back towards the adult bookstore.

Once I got there I went into the store with my things as I had a bag filled with the things that I will need to have while I am having sex in the gloryhole. As I got to the front counter the same young woman that was there before is still there. She nodded at me as in saying I am clear to go inside as she has already carded me before.

I then came up to her and I then said, "I would like to have one of the viewing rooms with a gloryhole."

"Ok, however you will need to rent a video in there." She said, to me with a smile.
I then looked to see what they have in terms of what they have to view, and I picked one as I did so I then paid her for the room which will be a total of 8 hours that I can be in the booth. After that I would either need to pay for another 8 hours or leave. However, the 8 hours should give me enough time to do what I came here to do.

Once I went into the booth, I saw that there is one hole or glory hole on my right hand side, and the other wall is whole with no gloryhole or any holes. There is a paper towel dispenser on the left side of the booth. In front of me, there is a screen with some controls as in volume, turn on and off, and that's about it, if I wanted to switch the movie I would have to head back in front and change it.

After a bit once I gotten myself ready, I then put my bag down on the floor and I made sure that the door behind me is locked, I then took out the things I needed, which is a small towel which I made sure I had, this will have my clothes on so they won't get soiled on the floor.

I placed it on the ground on the left side of the booth, as I then started to slowly get naked as I got naked, I placed my shoes onto the floor and the rest of my clothes onto the towel. Since I was wearing the lingerie that I had with me, I left it on me, only thing is my bottoms were off giving full access to my pussy and ass.

As I then prepared myself for the time when they will start coming, and since I got here first, and I am sure the other rooms, and spots have also been taken by either other slut wife's like myself or gay men who wish to have their asses fucked by random men.

After a bit of time, as I waited as I watched the video that I had playing, someone on the other side came and I then went over to the gloryhole as I watched who was on the other side, and it is a man. I then waited for him to see me first, and then once he does, I will see if he is interested in watching the porn video and jerking off to it or he could have sex with me, and I will allow him to cum inside of me.

So, after a bit of time once he got himself ready, I then asked, "Well babe, you can jerk off to what you're watching, or you could fuck me?"

He then turned to see me at the gloryhole which he was a bit surprise to see me, there and smiled as he then answered as he saw me, and said, "Sure I would love to fuck you instead."

"Let me suck your cock, that way I can make you nice and hard so you can fuck me deeply." I said, as I waited for him to stick his cock into the hole.

It didn't take long for him to do that, as he pulled his pants fully down and then he placed his cock into the hole, I then took his cock and I started to worship it with my tongue and mouth as I sucked on his cock, as I did so he started to grow larger in my mouth as I had him go as far down my throat as he could go down inside my mouth as he fucked my mouth.

I could hear as he grunted and moaned, then he reaches as large as he could as well as thick as he could, I then moved my face away from him as his cock is now completely out of my mouth. I then stood up and moved myself around as I did, I had a hold of his very wet, large and thick cock as I once I was ready guided it into my waiting pussy.

As his head of his cock was already in me, as he had no time to placed a condom on his cock, he is slowly going into me, as he slowly enters me, as he has started to already thrust in and out as he inches his way deeper inside of me. Soon he was as far into me as he could get, soon he started to fuck me harder and deeper as I panted and then I moaned.

"Oh yes fuck me, fuck me harder and deeper, oh God yes fuck me!" I said, as I panted and moan as he fucked me.

As I said that he obeyed and went as deep into my body as he could as he pounded me, while this is going on I have gotten more and more excited as I am having the first of many strangers fuck me hardcore. I knew at some point this man will come deep inside of me, making it very possible I could become pregnant with his child. However, I care less about that as I wanted to have him make me have his child, that would send my husband even more so turned on as he fucks me knowing that I am pregnant with someone else's child.

While he pounded my beautiful pussy, I started to squeeze on his cock in my pussy to give him a more tight feel as he pounded me, soon he started to moan and grunt as he was now plowing into me, telling me he knew how to fuck well, as even my husband has said when I squeeze on him that he says I felt very tight as if I was a virgin once more.

I then felt as he started to slow down a bit and then he started to pour his seed deep inside of my uterus, as I started to feel the first spasm of him coming in me, I soon started to come as well, which in turned made me started to roll my eyes back as I took my hands and held onto the other side of the wall, as I started to orgasm hard.

It didn't take him long before he finishes coming deep within me, and he slowly came out of me, I started to relax as I put my hands onto my stomach by my belly button, which is the part of my stomach without having any clothes on as my breast and above my belly button the lingerie covered.

I slowly moved away from the hole as I did my pussy burped loudly as the man's sperm dripped down to the floor. This was my first time having a stranger fuck me, I should feel a bit ashamed as I have never cheated on my husband, or anything but I don't.

Also, I didn't cheat on him as he knew fully well what I am doing, after a bit as the state of feeling bliss over what has just happened is still very fresh within my body, I then took some paper towels as I gentle wiped myself, making sure as much of it is inside of me as I could. I then sat back down onto the chair even though I could feel the wetness deep within my pussy.

I heard as the man in the other room, pulled his pants up and left the room, I smiled knowing I helped him out, as I hope to help others as well. After a bit I waited for the next person to come to the same room.

After a bit another person came into the room, and I then got up and did the same thing as I looked into the other room, I did this after I gave the person some time to get themselves ready etc.

Once I looked into the room, I smiled as it is another man. However, unlike last time he knew what is going on here, so he looked at the hole and I smiled as he saw me. He then pulled his pants down, revealing an already large and erected cock.

He went over to the hole, and he said, "I want to shove this into your pussy!"

"Can you come inside of me please?" I asked, him.

He then said to me, "Yes of course unless you want me to wear a condom."

I smiled as I got myself ready for him, as I had my ass against the wall as I did before, I then felt his large thick cock enter my pussy, as he got himself into me nice and slow at first he then started to pound into me, as he did so I put my hands to my stomach like I did, I could feel his cock deep inside of me as he pounded me hard.

Soon I started to scream in pleasure as my body is being used well, and it has yet to be ended, as he pounded me, he asked, "Do you like my cock into your body slut?"

"Oh God yes please fuck me, oh God you feel so good in my pussy, please fuck me and cum inside of me!" I answered him,

He then said, "Ah you are such a good little whore, I will for sure repay you for allowing me to fuck your wonderful pussy, I will indeed come deep in you, is that what you want my little slut?"

"Oh God yes!" I said, as I answered him.

He pounded me for a while then I could feel as he started to come deep in me, as I closed my eyes as he came deep in me. I didn't orgasm like I did before, but if he lasted a bit longer, I would have been able to come, however, for the next guy that fucks me he will have a surprise for sure when he will more likely to have me come maybe two times, I can sense I can more or less have more than one next time.

"Does that feel good for you, my little slut?" He asked me, as he finish what was left inside of me.

I then smiled as I answered him, "Fuck yes I needed to be used like this."

"Good to hear, well maybe next time I will have a bit more fun with you, but I need to take off, till next time." He said, as he pulled out of me, as he pulled his pants up and then left the room.

I then stepped away from the hole for a bit as I reached to get another paper towel as I wiped myself once more, as I did so, I tried my hardest to place as much of the newly fresh cum into me, but he came a lot inside of my wanting cunt.

I now have a choice, do I stay here and get more men to come inside of me or do I get myself ready and head back home and call it quits as I have now had two men fuck me tonight, do I want to have more or do I want to stay here and get more men to come deep inside of my pussy? Either way I should choose now, before the next man comes and see's that I am not ready.

I then said out loud, "Fuck it, I want more cum inside of me."

I said it in a way that no one else could really make out what I said, unless if they were in the booth with me, which kind of gave me an idea but this will happened later on and not today. I then sat down once more to be ready for the next man to show up.

As I sat back down my ass is now used to the cold seat of the chair that is in here, I wishes it was cushion, but I understand why, it would be too much of a pain in the neck to keep cleaning and too expensive to keep replacing. So, I will wait till the next man to show up, however I have now considered that after this next one I will call it quits and head back home I am starting to get a bit tired.

So as I sat on the chair that is in the booth, I waited for the next person to enter the same room, that the other two men were in, as I slowly rolled my head back, as I closed my eyes as I could still feel the warm sperm inside of my uterus as it is deep inside of me, while I have my eyes shut and my head back towards the ceiling I have my hands on my naked belly button, as I wait for the sound from the room next door to me.

I then heard the sound of the door opening up slowly next door to me, as I then opened up my eyes as well as leveled my head as I then slowly turned my head towards the gloryhole which has been used now by me twice, the source of such joy and pleasure as I looked I then got up and went over to it, as I then stared into the room on the other side till I see the next person, on the other side. My concern is this, as simple as it sounds, will I have another woman on the other side thinking there is a man here, or a gay man wanted his ass fucked.

However, as I watched on my side, I soon found that another man came into the room. One by the sound and sight of him, tells me this is no gay man, but straight, one which more then likely would love to fuck a free pussy, and bury his cock inside of me, and then spill his seed deep inside of my nice warm body.

I waited as I did my body prepared for another feeling of a nice large invader within my body, as such my body prepared to have more then one orgasm, the one that should have been with the man before and with this man as well.

As he got himself ready, and then he looked at the hole, he smiled but he didn't seem to see me, but smiled as if he expected to find someone soon on the other side. I wondered should I allow myself to be known or should I just relax and let things happened.

I then said, to myself, "Fuck it, I will announce I am here."

So, I did so, as I then looked at him and I asked, "Do you want to have a nice pussy, or do you wish to jerk off alone?"

The man didn't seemed surprise at all, and turned towards me, as he was already putting his pants down, and he said, "I knew you were there I saw you, that is why I have yet to turn on the TV. But yes, I would love to fuck you."

"Ah so you did see me then, well do you want me to blow you, or do you want my pussy?" I asked him, wanting to make sure I please him.

He then pulled his pants all the way down and said, "I will have your pussy."

I then went over to the hole once more as I got myself ready as he slides his cock into me, he has a larger cock then most as he started to fuck me deep and slow, soon he said to me, "Damn you are tight, but I can tell you had some action already."

"Thank you." I said as I panted as he fucked me nice and slow.

He then started to pound me as he I could tell is liking my tight pussy, as he did my pants turned to moans, then soon I started to let out screams as I once more orgasm, as I orgasm he slowly fucked me, giving me time to fully orgasm, and once I was done he went back to pounding my cunt harder and faster.

This in turned caused me to orgasm again, but a bit later after I came the first time with him, as he fucked me good, I moaned loudly, or I scream with the sound and music of a women being fucked well.

It didn't take long for him to also come inside of my already filled up womb, as his seed shot straight inside of me, as it did I felt the warm of his semen, as it made its way to my uterus, as this happened I had both hands on my stomach as I felt him even now as he keeps thrusting inside of me. Sending me more and more over the edge as I once more came, after he came inside of me, he keeps fucking me.

Then once his cock had enough, he came once more inside of me, which sent me into a much more powerful orgasm. At which time he then slowly came out of me, after he finish deep inside of me. At that point, I have no considered to now call it a night and head home as I had my fill for the night. Any more would leave me too sore to do anything else.

I stayed like I was till I heard him get dress and as he did so I felt as my pussy allowed a lot of the cum to dripped down onto the floor below, which already has had its fair share of cum from the other men from before.

Once he was dress and left the room, I then moved myself, as I did my legs were sore from what I did. Once I was able to move once more, I then used a towel and wiped myself up, I then took out what I had with me and cleaned myself up as well as I could.

I then afterwards got dress, as I gathered up my things as I then left the room and headed back to the front. I then let the clerk up front that I was done and which room that I was in. I then left the store and headed back to my car. Once I got to my car, I entered it as I did so I place my bag on the passenger's seat and I took off.

On the way home, I wonder what else should I do, as I started to once more get horny again. As I was on my way home I saw a local park that I started to wonder if people have sex in it, as I have heard some people do.

The End